Janisch/Blau
The Fantastic Adventures of Baron Munchausen

Munchausen statue in St. Petersburg (erected 1782).

Heinz Janisch

The Fantastic Adventures of Baron Munchausen

Traditional and Newly Discovered

Tales of

Karl Friedrich Hieronymus von Munchausen

With illustrations by Aljoscha Blau

Translated by Belinda Cooper

ENCHANTED LION BOOKS

NEW YORK

FOREWORD

It is widely believed that the adventurer and "Baron of Lies" Munchausen, about whom numerous books have been written and films have been made, is an invention. But Karl Friedrich Hieronymus von Munchausen really lived.

He was born on May 11, 1720, and died on February 22, 1797, at the age of 77 in the German town of Bodenwerder on the Weser. Even in his own lifetime, in 1781, a collection of stories about his many amazing adventures was published. The librarian Rudolf Erich Raspe (1737-1794) and the writer Gottfried August Bürger (1747-1794) guaranteed Baron Munchausen's immortality by recording and documenting his many adventures and experiences.

But very few know that on March 12, 1778, Baron Munchausen arrived in Vienna by coach after a long and difficult journey . He came at the invitation of Count Zweritzky, whom he had met the year before in Weimar.

On the day of his arrival, Munchausen was the guest of honor at a dinner held at the Count's palace. The Baron's travels through Europe were already well known, and he had long since gained renown. It therefore was not surprising that after dinner, to the delight of the guests, the Count asked Munchausen to relate some tales from his life.

The next day the *Vienna Illustrated Paper* reported that, "the Baron acquitted himself in a dramatic voice while standing at the table and gesticulating wildly, to the great delight of his audience."

Baron Munchausen spent the next nine days in Vienna. As he described it in a letter, he stayed at the home of Count Nepomuk, a friend of Count Zweritzky. Over those nine days he recorded some of his adventures in a small notebook. He seems to have begun these notes earlier in St. Petersburg as the notation "In St. Petersburg" can be found on the first page of his book, while "In Vienna" is only at the top of page 17.

On his departure he left this notebook with Count Nepomuk, most likely with the request that it be presened to Count Zweritzky in gratitude for his invitation. But Count Nepomuk died in a riding accident only two days after Munchausen's departure, and the little book was completely forgotten. This explains why it never found its way into the hands of the Zweritzky family and turned up only 200 years later in a trunk in the attic of a house on Siebenstern Lane in Vienna's 7th District. The photographer who lived there, Emanuel S., left me this trunk of old books and notebooks as a thank-you gift for helping him move his belongings.

In addition to a lovely, valuable edition of Adalbert Stifter's *Indian Summer*, I thus came into possession of this precious, slender notebook in which Carl Friedrich Hieronymus von Munchausen recounts adventures both familiar and — to me — completely unfamiliar. I thank my publisher for accepting my invitation to publish a selection of these stories, and for finding the painter Aljoscha Blau, born in St. Petersburg, to do the illustrations, thus closing the St. Petersburg-Vienna circle 200 years later.

Heinz Janisch
Vienna, February 2007

The notebook containing Munchausen's handwritten notes is accompanied by a letter that I would not wish to withhold from you, my dear readers.

Vienna, March, 1778

Honorable Count!

The pheasant yesterday was once again superb when it arrived in such timely fashion on your richly set table. In order to gratify your grace with a stroke of my own, I have dipped my pen in ink and have proceeded, for the sake of pure pleasure, to write down some of what I related at the table over the last few days. Thus my pages, like well-seasoned, tasty pheasants, fly to your grace with the best of thanks, and I do believe – by my pigtail! – that they will be to your liking! With great esteem and my sincerest greetings to your honorable wife, your four lively children, and Poldi the poodle!

Carl Friedrich Hieronymus von Münchhausen

The Horse on the Church Roof

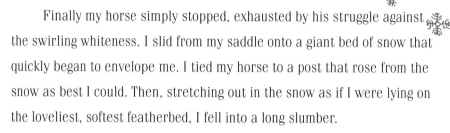

I mounted my horse and rode straight into winter. It was snowing more heavily than anything I had ever seen! It was as if the sky was hurling not just snowflakes but whole clouds down upon me. Since I was on my way to Russia I had to get through this endless winter, like it or not. But strangely enough, I felt as if I were not so much moving forward as plowing deeper and deeper into the white ground.

Finally my horse simply stopped, exhausted by his struggle against the swirling whiteness. I slid from my saddle onto a giant bed of snow that quickly began to envelope me. I tied my horse to a post that rose from the snow as best I could. Then, stretching out in the snow as if I were lying on the loveliest, softest featherbed, I fell into a long slumber.

I slept so soundly that I did not awake until the sun was already high in the sky. When I opened my eyes I found myself lying in a square in front of a church, surrounded by old stone houses. How could this be? Was I dreaming? Could I really be awake? As for my horse, I looked around for him but he seemed to have disappeared completely.

Then I heard a whinnying up in the sky, as if my horse were flying through the air above me. And so he was, or almost! Up there, beneath the dome of the sky, hung my horse! He was tied to the church steeple by a leather strap, and the poor thing was flopping around and whinnying, trying his best to come down and join me on solid ground.

Only then did I understand it all! The sun had melted the snow and the post I had seen the day before must have been the church steeple. Without a second thought, I aimed my pistol. With a single shot, I snapped the leather strap in two and my horse landed on all fours next to me, safe and sound.

After a brief greeting, we flew like an arrow out of the village.

The Battle of the White Feathers

Although I have traveled through many countries as a soldier, I pride myself on the fact that I have never shot at anyone. Fighting on the battlefield always seemed quite foolish to me. I therefore was particularly delighted once in Russia when everyone forgot to fight from sheer laughter. One day, when a new battle was imminent, I decided it was time to bring the constant shooting to an end. Having come up with a plan, I set about obtaining large sacks of goose feathers from a peasant. Then, once night had fallen, I snuck with my sacks, which were as light as air, into the enemy army's camp. Luckily, the foreign soldiers had eaten and drunk plentifully, as had our own, so they slept soundly and no one noticed my nighttime visit.

I began by rolling their cannon balls down the hill, one by one, as I already had done with our own. Then I stuffed as many feathers as I could into three or four cannons and disarmed the others. I had already filled our own cannons with feathers. Then I slipped silently back to camp and allowed myself a few hours of sleep.

The morning began with a wake up call on the trumpet, and a few minutes later the first shots were fired.

But they sounded different from usual. More muffled; and no cannonballs came shooting out on either side. Instead, white feathers floated down upon us. It was snowing goose feathers, hundreds and thousands of them! Some got into people's uniforms, others into their noses. Here and there soldiers began to laugh as feathers tickled them in sensitive spots. Others couldn't stop sneezing, and soon enough all these soldiers were sitting on the ground laughing so hard they were holding their sides.

Their laughter was contagious. All over the battlefield people started to giggle and laugh, and everywhere there were feathers swirling silently through the air. No one thought of fighting any more.

I watched the merrymaking on the battlefield for a while. Then, blowing a few small feathers from my mouth, I made my way, thirsty but greatly satisfied, to the nearest inn.

It is said that even many long years later soldiers still told of the famous "battle of the white feathers."

The Ride on the Cannon Ball

I have ridden on all sorts of marvelous creatures, such as a greyhound that carried me rapidly through the countryside, and a polar bear that kept my feet from freezing on the arctic ice. I have been pulled through the air by wild geese and even flown to the moon on a beanstalk. But of all my journeys, one was stranger by far than all the others.

Believe it or not, I once rode on a cannonball, and I must say that I never traveled like that before or since!

As it happened, we had laid siege to a city, and I had been chosen to do a little spying. This, however, was easier said than done, for the city walls were very high and guards were posted everywhere.

Either I could enter the city from below by digging myself in, or I could come from above through the air.

As I was considering my situation, a cannon was fired, probably as a warning, not far from where I was standing. On an impulse I flung myself onto the flying cannonball. I held tight and felt the wind rush into my face. As I flew I wondered how I would get back out of the fortress, but only for a moment, for I suddenly realized that rescue was already in sight.

As one of the enemy's cannonballs flew past me towards our camp, I leapt in midair from my cannonball onto the other, and in no time I was flying back to safety. Then, at just the right moment, I leaped, quite elegantly I must say, from the enemy cannonball, landing safely on the ground. Meanwhile, the cannonball I had just abandoned sped off and crashed in a far away field.

Fortunately, I had seen enough from my airy perch to be able to give a detailed report of the fortress. My task accomplished, I took myself off to recover from my unusual trip through the air.

The Miraculous Rescue from the Marsh

On some days one leaps easily through life, as though there were springs beneath one's feet. One lovely summer's day, blessed with a good mood, my beloved horse and I managed the best trick of all. We rode up to a passing coach and, to the great astonishment of the ladies traveling within, we jumped in through one of the coach's open windows and out through the other. If truth be told, I even managed to remove my hat in the friendliest of greetings.

Being in fine form, I then rode up one side of the nearest tree, plucked some sweet fruits and rode down the other side of the trunk. As I galloped past the coach, I flung a few of these choice sweets into the laps of the noble ladies.

I galloped faster and faster through the countryside. When a river crossed our path, my horse and I forgot all about the bridge before us, and we jumped straight over the sparkling water in a single bound.

Yet even miracle horses get tired.

During a daring leap over an enormous marsh that suddenly appeared before us, my horse's energy flagged. As the swamp beneath us grew bigger and bigger, we both suddenly landed in the mud with tremendous force. In seconds my horse and I had sunk down up to our necks, and I thought our time had come.

Fortunately, by some miracle, right at that moment I remembered what my old grandmother had often told me: "Sometimes you have to pull yourself up by your own hair in order not to go under!" Taking hold of my pigtail, I pulled on it as hard as I could. I pulled with my knees pressed firmly against my horse's back, and with enormous effort I was able to pull us slowly out of the swamp.

After a short rest on dry land I mounted my horse once again and, with a single bound over a low-flying owl, we leaped into our next adventure.

The Earth Turner

In my travels through many lands, I have had occasion to strike up relationships with many unusual companions. I even owe my life to some of them. Once a small man, whose name I do not know and whom I therefore will simply call the Earth Turner, saved me from an extremely dangerous situation.

I had traveled by a roundabout way to a land whose customs were completely strange to me. The inhabitants of this country lived in trees and threw all sorts of things at anyone who came their way. Fruits, stones, even whole chests and chairs came flying at me.

Seeking protection inside a rocky enclosure, I encountered another traveler – a small friendly man with astonishingly large feet. "These people clearly want to be left alone," he muttered to himself. I could only agree.

"It's probably best to get away from here as quickly as possible," I said. "But how are we to do that without half the sky falling on our heads?"

"Let me worry about that," said the small man. Then he took me by the arm and with a powerful swing, he threw me over his broad shoulders.

"Hold tight," he cried, and he began to run in place like mad, without moving one inch from the spot. This small man ran and ran, his legs going faster and faster, until I got dizzy from watching them. But then, to my surprise, the earth began to turn slowly beneath his feet. As he ran, his large feet turned the earth — slowly at first, then faster and faster. Rivers, lakes, huge forests, fields and lush meadows all rushed by, and I even saw the desert beneath his feet.

Then, without slowing down at all, this unusual man stood still. Having turned the entire earth with his feet, he wasn't even out of breath. "Here we are," he said with satisfaction. He lifted me from his shoulders and set me down on solid ground. "This is the way to Germany," he said pointing. "I have to go in the other direction." After bowing and thanking him, I said, "Please allow me one question: Where did you learn to do that?" The Earth Turner looked at me and laughed with delight. "Oh, I could do it even as a child," he cried, and with a few steps he had disappeared among the trees.

A Sack Full of Sunshine

Only a few weeks after my encounter with the Earth Turner, I met a woman who also amazed me with her unusual talent. This happened in a forest near the border between Prussia and Austria. Some travel companions and I had lost our way, and we wandered through the bushes until — at last! — we found ourselves in a small clearing in front of a house. At our knocks and cries, a friendly woman opened the door and welcomed us as though we were old friends. As it was growing dark outside, we asked her about sleeping quarters. Our hostess told us that her husband and two sons had just returned from chopping wood, but that there was an empty hut only a few steps away into the woods and that we could sleep there. "But you'll want to take a sack of light with you," she continued as she placed a bulging sack at my feet, adding that it contained sunlight she had gathered herself. "It's quite dark in the woods," she said, knowingly.

I almost laughed out loud in disbelief, but instead, with a quick cough and a "thank you," we went on our way.

The sack was as light as an empty shirt. We marched through the undergrowth and soon reached the hut, in which we found a small amount of straw and wood. But the woman had been right! It quickly got so dark in the woods and in our hut that we couldn't see our own hands and feet. Without a second thought, I placed the sack in the middle of the room and opened it. Lo and behold! Golden sunshine streamed forth from the sack filling the room with light! The sack was stuffed to the brim with sunbeams! The sunlight shone for us all through the night, but by early morning it was all used up. Leaving the hut, we soon found a path that led us out of the woods.

I have often heard of people who would like to keep sunlight in a dark sack, but no one has ever succeeded in doing so, other than the woman in the woods who gave us that precious gift.

I still have the empty sack, but to this day I have never succeeded in gathering sunshine.

Should I find myself in that wood again, I shall visit the friendly light gatherer and ask for her advice.

The Journey to Egypt

I have traveled over much of my life, though not always voluntarily. Once I found myself in a Turkish jail as a prisoner of war. Since I had achieved a degree of fame from my adventures, the soldiers brought me before the Sultan of Constantinople. The Sultan soon had great confidence in me and entrusted me with some delicate undertakings.

One day the Sultan sent me on a secret mission to Egypt. He gave me a sealed letter that I was to bring straight to a friend in Cairo.

I set off at once with my companions. After a little while we saw a short lanky man running across a field. From each leg he dragged a heavy iron ball.

"Where to, my friend?" I called to him. "And what are those balls for?"

The man sighed. "I just ran out of Vienna half an hour ago, and I'm already approaching Constantinople! I drag these weights around so I won't get everywhere too early!"

I liked the man, and since I had need of a fast runner, I took him into my service.

Half an hour later I saw a man lying in the grass with one ear to the ground.

"What is there to hear, my friend?" I asked him pleasantly.

"I'm listening to the grass grow!" said the man. "It's a nice way to pass the time."

"We also have a lot to listen to," I said, and asked the man to join us.

Soon after we met a man who was shooting his musket into the air, straight into the empty sky.

"What are you shooting at, my friend?" I asked curiously, since not a bird was to be seen.

"Oh, a sparrow was sitting on the church spire in Strasbourg, and since that won't do, I frightened it away."

"I'd like a sharpshooter like you," I said, and in no time we had a new brave companion among us.

Together we traveled through many cities and countries.

In the mountains of Lebanon, a man approached us, pulling an entire forest behind him on a rope.

"What are you pulling there, my friend?" I asked the stalwart fellow.

"Oh, I wanted to gather firewood, but I forgot my axe at home. So I had to find another way!"

With these words, he snapped a tree trunk in half as though it were a reed. I also invited this strong man to join us.

When we arrived in Egypt a terrible storm arose, which spun us all through the air as though we were mere blades of grass.

Looking around, I noticed a fat man standing in a nearby field. He was pinching his right nostril closed with his forefinger, and with his left nostril he was creating a powerful wind. When he saw us fighting the storm from his nose, he stopped blowing and bowed before us. The wind ceased immediately.

"What are you doing there, my friend?" I asked angrily.

"Pardon me, your Excellency!" the man replied apologetically. "I just wanted to make some wind for the seven windmills over there. I kept one nostril closed so as not to blow them over entirely."

This windmaker, too, I asked to accompany us.

Together we arrived swiftly and safely in Cairo, and I passed on the Sultan's letter. With that, my secret mission was accomplished.

But my five new friends — the fast runner, the grass listener, the sharpshooter, the strongman and the windmaker — stayed with me. This would prove most helpful in many a sticky situation to come.

The Wager with the Sultan

The Sultan of Constantinople loved to hear my stories. We often sat together for hours while he listened to me tell of my adventures.

During one of these evenings he served his best wine and told me that no finer wine could be found in all the world.

"By your leave, noble Sultan," I said. "The Empress of Vienna, Maria Theresa, has some bottles of Hungarian Tokay in her cellars. One sip and you will cry with joy! If you like, I can obtain a bottle of this wine in only an hour! If it hasn't arrived by the time the hour is up, you can chop off my head. What's the use of a head if it can only tell lies?"

"That is a high price to pay," said the Sultan. "But I accept your wager. If the wine is on my table in an hour, you will be richly rewarded."

I went immediately into the garden and summoned the fast runner who had joined me during my trip to Egypt.

I wrote a letter to the Empress, whom I knew well, and begged her to give my messenger a bottle of her excellent wine. I wrote that it was a matter of life and death!

The fast runner removed the weights that he needed to keep him from shooting off at any moment like an arrow and arriving at the ends of the earth in no time. Once released, he flew off with my letter, and I knew that he would be standing before me again in no time. I calmly took a seat by the Sultan and waited, but time passed and my fast runner did not return.

"Another five minutes, my dear friend," said the Sultan gaily, and he summoned a man with the largest saber I had ever seen in my life. I began to feel a little queasy, so I called for my second companion, the grass listener. He laid his ear to the ground in the garden and said, "Our man is lying in a meadow snoring. I can hear it from here."

I asked my third friend, the sharpshooter, to do something quickly. After all, my head was important and dear to me. The sharpshooter picked up his musket and said, "I see him. He's lying under a tree sleeping, and there's a bottle next to him."

With one shot he hit a bough full of nuts. As it split apart, the nuts rained down on the fast runner. He started up, dazed, but seeing the bottle, he took it and in a moment he stood before me.

The Sultan had eyes only for the wine. Taking a sip, he gave me a long look, and finally began to cry. So I hadn't lied after all!

"I'm crying with joy," said the Sultan, wiping tears from his face. "Just as you said I would! This imperial wine from Vienna gladdens my palate and my heart!"

The noble bottle brought me luck as well.

"Take as much from my treasury as a man can carry," said the Sultan as he poured another glass of wine.

I called my fourth companion, the strongman, who could carry tree

trunks in his hands like blades of grass. Reaching into the Sultan's treasury with both hands, he filled them with so much of the Sultan's vast treasure that when he was done only a single silver coin remained.

"The Sultan won't like this!" I thought to myself.

At the harbor we bought the first ship we came upon. The fifth of my trusty friends, the windmaker, also came aboard, and we quickly took leave with our treasures.

As I had feared, the Sultan soon sent his entire fleet after us. But the windmaker simply pinched one of his nostrils closed and with the other he blew all the ships back into the harbor as though they were mere toys. Then he pointed a nostril at our sails and soon a mighty storm drove us out onto the open sea.

We set our course for Italy. Once there, we divided the silver coins among ourselves and settled in for a time.

After a while my companions decided to try their luck in the countryside. As for myself, I was soon drawn back to the open sea.

The Concert in the Whale

I have always loved to sail the seas in a boat, which for me is much like a wooden horse, and to steer towards new islands and dangers. One morning while sailing on the high seas, I heard music coming from somewhere. I looked around, but there wasn't a ship in sight. Still, there was no doubt that the wonderful music was coming from the sea!

"Someone is playing the piano under water!" I cried delightedly.

At that moment a giant whale surfaced quite close to me, and I could hear that the music came from inside of him.

Without taking time to think, I leapt into the huge sea creature's mouth just as he took a breath. Once inside the whale, I simply followed the music. And it was true! In the whale's huge belly, lighted by candles, stood a piano. A young man in a white shirt skimmed his fingers over the keys.

"You play quite excellently!" I said with a bow.

"Thank you," answered the young man politely. "Do you also play an instrument?"

"Almost all of them," I replied, for as a child I had enjoyed the best musical education.

The young man pointed to a harp that I hadn't noticed before, inviting me to join him. I readied myself, and together we played a most lovely duet.

"This must be a musical whale," I said as other musicians began to arrive with their instruments. We all made music together for what I can only imagine was a long time.

"Wouldn't you like to play on my ship?" I asked after the last notes had died away.

"Another time," said the man at the piano, and the others nodded at me pleasantly in agreement. "Here we have all the quiet in the world, and no other concert hall sounds nearly as good as this one!"

I listened for a while longer before taking my leave and making my way back up. At a favorable moment I jumped from the mouth of the musical creature, landing safely back on the deck of my ship.

Before I could recount my experiences to my mates, my friends in the whale's belly began to play again. Their playing was such a joy to hear that all we could do was listen. We let our ship glide along beside the whale and his orchestra through the ocean without doing a single thing. Sitting on deck, we let the wind drive us. As the beautiful music carried over the water, we sat transfixed.

Thus it was that the music and the waves carried us into our next adventure.

The Vanishing Sea

I have experienced many things on my journeys by ship — good things and terrible things, as well as mighty storms with waves as high as mountains that put the fear of God in me. But the most unusual thing that ever happened was when the sea beneath our bow disappeared completely. We were enjoying ourselves, sailing from one island to another, when we noticed that the water carrying our ship was becoming lower and lower with every passing hour. As we looked around we noticed that a whale and some other sea creatures were already lying on nearly dry land. Clearly it was high time to get to the bottom of things in the truest sense of the word!

Upon investigation, I found a huge hole in the ground into which all the water seemed to be disappearing. Nearby on the sand lay a large stone plate with a knob in the middle. Apparently someone had pulled the stopper out of the sea, and now the whole ocean was in danger of draining away.

I returned to my companions and explained what had happened and what we had to do. With great effort, we dragged the heavy stopper back into place. Now the water could no longer drain out of the sea, but we had to wait a full three days before the first raindrops fell. It rained for seven days and seven nights without stopping. Slowly the sea began to rise again. We watched gratefully as all the fish began to disappear into its dark blue depths.

We sailed on happily, satisfied that we had saved the sea and all its inhabitants.

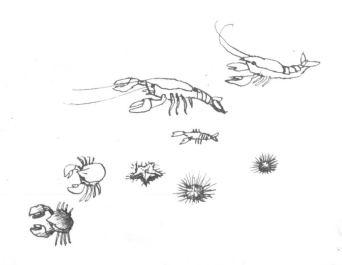

The Ride on the Seahorse

It is to my father and his miraculous slingshot that I owe my discovery of precious sea fruits at the bottom of the ocean.

My father must have been a brave man for it was the Russian Czar himself, or so they say, who presented him with his magic slingshot. According to legend, this same slingshot was once used by little David against the great Goliath. To my joy and satisfaction, my father passed this miracle slingshot on to me and, as you might imagine, it has often proved most helpful.

One day, for example, while I was having dinner with an English lord in London, a bomb suddenly flew threw the open window and landed right in the middle of the table. Without a minute to lose, I brought out my magic slingshot and in seconds had shot the burning sphere so high into the sky that when it exploded all we could see was the shimmering of a thousand tiny pieces. Believe it or not, many of the silver stars we now see in the night sky are shards from that very evening.

On another occasion, when I had been in a big city for a while and suddenly had a yearning to see the ocean, I simply pulled myself taut in the slingshot, and soon I had landed on the soft sand of a spectacular beach. Curiously, I didn't land directly on the sand, but in a saddle without a horse that someone must have forgotten on the beach. Without hesitation, I stepped with it into the water.

Before long I found myself face to face with a seahorse, and in no time at all I had my saddle over his back. My new horse and I were ready to roam.

Many people don't believe that seahorses can grow as big as the horses in our fields, but they can, I assure you. I not only have seen this with my own eyes, but I have ridden one of them as well!

Fortunately, my father had taught me how to hold my breath under water for hours, so I had no trouble riding my seahorse slowly through the water. As I did so, I gazed in astonishment at all the things I was discovering on the bottom of the sea.

I passed palaces made entirely of fire and elaborate sandcastles built by fish parents and their children. I saw towers of transparent glass inhabited by unusually long fish. In a coral theater, I listened to a chorus of fish singing sad songs of nets and fishing boats. My trusty seahorse brought me safely through all of the crevices. Finally, we saw an elegant woman who appeared to be asleep in a chair, comfortably perched on the sea floor.

I woke her cautiously and offered her a seat on the back of my seahorse, which she accepted gratefully. She told me that she had fallen asleep while taking a stroll through the sea. I later found out from her friends that she had been asleep under water for three years.

I must admit that I was much taken with this inhabitant from the bottom of the sea. Thus, when she asked me after only seven days on dry land whether she might accompany me, I already knew where our journey would take us.

We took two chairs and disappeared into the ocean. How long did we stay there? And what did we experience at the bottom of the sea? I'll tell you about it another time – perhaps.

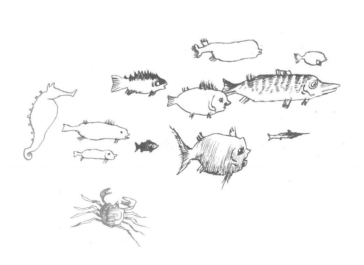

For Emanuel. H. J.

For Zacharie. And thank you to all of those who took up my invitation to ride with the Baron: Heinz, Heike, Ute and Torsten. A. B.

www.enchantedlionbooks.com

First American Edition published in 2010 by
Enchanted Lion Books LLC, 20 Jay Street, Studio M-18, Brooklyn, NY 11201

Originally published in Germany as *Der Ritt auf dem Seepferd*
by Heinz Janisch, illustrated by Aljoscha Blau.

© Aufbau Verlag GmbH & Co. KG, Berlin 2007
Negotiated by Aufbau Media GmbH, Berlin

Translation © 2009 by Enchanted Lion Books, LLC

ISBN 978-1-59270-091-2

Printed in February 2010 in China by South China Printing Co., Ltd., King Yip (Dong Guan) Printing & Packaging
Factory Co.,Ltd., Daning Administrative District, Humen Town, Dong Guan City, Guangdong Province 523930